A Barrel Racer's Dream

By M.D. Ford

Illustrated by Harry Aveira

ROCKING HORSE RODEO

Whispering Horse Books, LLC

ACKNOWLEDGEMENTS

A special thank you to the wonderful professionals
that helped me through this process.

Bobbie Hinman, Editor
April M. Cox, Coaching & Project Management
Praise Saflor, Graphic Designer
Lyda Mclallen, Marketing/PR Consultant

Publisher's Cataloging-in-Publication Data

Names: Ford, M. D., author. | Aveira, Harry, illustrator.
Title: A Barrel Racer's Dream / M.D. Ford ; illustrated by Harry Aveira.
Series: Rocking Horse Rodeo
Description: Mesa, AZ: Whispering Horse Books, LLC, 2020. | Summary: Dee loves the
rodeo and dreams of becoming a good barrel racer.
Identifiers: LCCN: 2020904409 | ISBN: 978-1-7346389-0-5 (Hardcover) | 978-1-
7346389-1-2 (pbk.) | 978-1-7346389-2-9 (activity) | 978-1-7346389-3-6 (ebook)
Subject: LCSH Horses--Juvenile fiction. | Friendship--Juvenile fiction. | Barrel
racing--Fiction. | Rodeos--Juvenile fiction. | Imagination--Juvenile fiction. | CYAC
Horses--Fiction. | Friendship--Fiction. | Barrel racing--Fiction. | Rodeos--Fiction. |
Imagination--fiction. | BISAC JUVENILE FICTION / Imagination & Play | JUVENILE
FICTION / Lifestyles / Farm & Ranch Life | JUVENILE FICTION / Animals / Horses
Classification: LCC PZ7.1.F659 Ba 2020 | DDC [E]--dc23

DEDICATION

To a rootin', tootin' cowgirl,
full of life and the love of horses.
Sharon Angus Dodgen Wright.
A horse trainer of Western Horsemanship,
Showmanship and Trail,
and a friend.

To my best friend and horse, Hank.
He brought me more joy than one can only imagine.
Yee-haw!

"I'm going to ride
in a rodeo today!
Yippee!"

4

Dee is excited. She has always dreamed
of riding her horse, Hank, in a rodeo.
Hank is not only her horse, he's also her very best friend.
Dee imagines entering all sorts of adventurous rodeo events.
To her, the most exciting one of all is BARREL RACING!

Today her dreams will come true.

Dee hurries out to the stable to get Hank ready for their exciting day. She brushes him until his coat shines in the morning sun.

She cleans his hooves, then wraps his legs to protect them on the ride to the arena. Hank is excited, too. He eagerly walks up the ramp and into the trailer.

Dee gathers the tack and other equipment
they will need for the day.

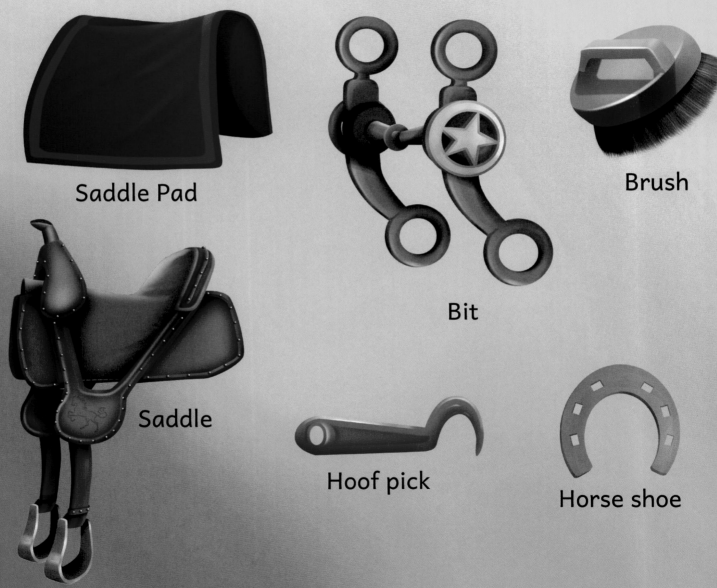

Saddle Pad

Bit

Brush

Saddle

Hoof pick

Horse shoe

Then, she jumps in the truck and off they go to the rodeo.

When they arrive, they see many other horses and riders hustling and bustling. Everyone is busy getting their horses ready. Lots of other people have also come to watch the rodeo.

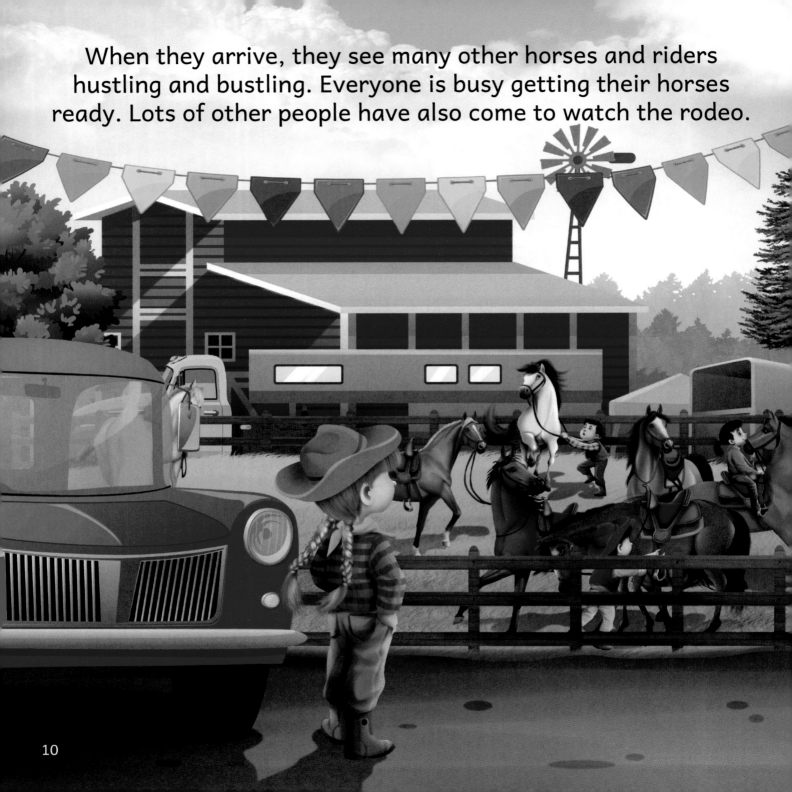

Dee unloads Hank from the trailer and dresses him in his saddle and bridle. She looks into Hank's big brown eyes and knows that he is ready. She climbs up onto his back... and they are ready to go.

They take their place in line.

When it's their turn, they proudly enter the big arena.

12

Dee and Hank can feel each other shivering with excitement as they see the barrels. All they need to do is ride as fast as they can around each barrel and then race back across the finish line. The barrels are arranged in a cloverleaf pattern, so Dee will have to guide Hank carefully. She pats him on his neck.

It's their turn to ride.

"Good boy, Hank," she says. "We can do this."
Together they can do it. After all, they are best friends.

As Hank turns toward the barrels, Dee loosens the reins. This is Hank's signal to get ready to race. Then Dee taps him gently with her legs, and Hank is off in a flash. He reaches the first barrel, turning tightly to the right.

Dee taps him again to guide him as they turn and head for the next one. This time they have to turn left.

Then they race around the last barrel, make another left turn and head for the finish line. Dee lets the reins drop onto Hank's neck, then leans forward and lets him fly! What a ride!

The energy and freedom...
and the wind in her hair!

They did it! The crowd is cheering.

Dee walks Hank around the grounds to cool him off after his hard work. She thanks him over and over again for being her best friend. They are a team.

Dee and Hank watch as the other riders take turns racing around the barrels. Dee remembers the many hours of practice and the time it took to become good at this event. She loves the thrill of the competition and the fun of doing it with her best friend.

Dee hopes that she and Hank are the winners, but she also knows it is important to be a good sport, whether she wins or not.

The announcer enters the arena holding a beautiful blue ribbon. Dee stretches her arms around Hank's neck as they listen for the name of the winning team. The announcer's voice comes over the loud speaker.

"The blue ribbon goes to..."

"Dee and Hank!"

With tears of joy, Dee rides Hank into the arena to collect their ribbon. Dee congratulates all of the other participants. They did a great job, too.

The exciting day has come to a happy end.
Dee cleans up, loads the truck, and heads for home.

Later that evening, Dee smiles as she remembers the rodeo.

Most of all, she remembers how she and Hank worked together as a team to win the race. Hank really is her best friend.

"I will do all this for real someday," she says.

"I will have to practice,

practice, practice,

but I know I can do it."

Dee picks up the reins and off they go—
she and her rocking horse.

What lessons can we learn from barrel racing?

- ✓ Balance and movement.
- ✓ Strength in partnering with your horse.
- ✓ Confidence and skill.
- ✓ Friendship and Love.
- ✓ Practice, practice, practice.
- ✓ Levels of professional barrel racing.

The Cloverleaf Pattern

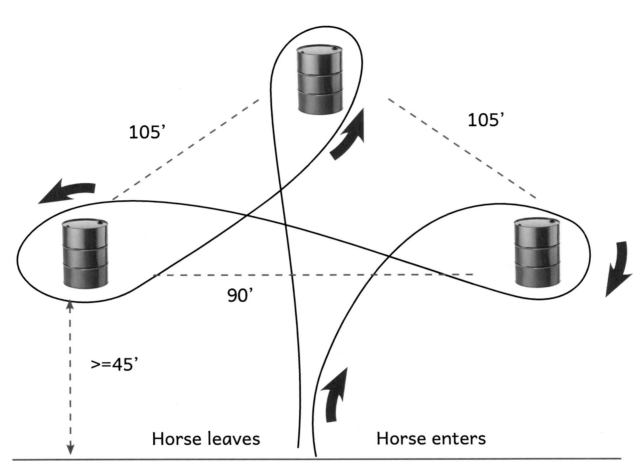

105'

105'

90'

>=45'

Horse leaves

Horse enters

*Flag and Timer are needed to have accuracy.

Visit our web site at www.whisperinghorsebooks.com for more barrel racing resources, web sites and tips.

About the Author

M. D. Ford grew up on a horse farm with many other animals. Before she was allowed to ride a horse, she had to learn every aspect of it first, from feeding, washing, to leading. She had to do the groundwork and learn how to take care of a horse before she was allowed to ride one. But it didn't take M. D. Ford long, and she started riding by the time she was five.

At the age of seven, M. D. Ford started competing. Her first competition was an egg race, where she also won her first trophy. Her first competition on a horse was Barrel Racing. During the race, she had three barrels to run around with her horse. Her second horse, Hank, could run around the barrels by himself.

M. D. Ford grew up at the Rodeo with her family. She has won over 500 ribbons and 250 trophies while also getting covered in dirt and hitting her knees on the barrels.

About the Illustrator

Harry Aveira has been creating children's books for twenty years with more than a hundred books (and counting). He loves partnering with authors to help bring their stories to life. Harry lives in Indonesia with his two daughters and his wife.

A GIFT FOR YOU WITH OUR THANKS

Visit us at www.rockinghorserodeo.com to sign up for our VIP list and get a FREE copy of our activity book.

If you loved the book, visit Amazon.com or Goodreads.com to help us spread the word! Thank you in advance!

Made in the USA
Middletown, DE
15 December 2021

54268951R00022